THE LONG WAY
WESTWARD

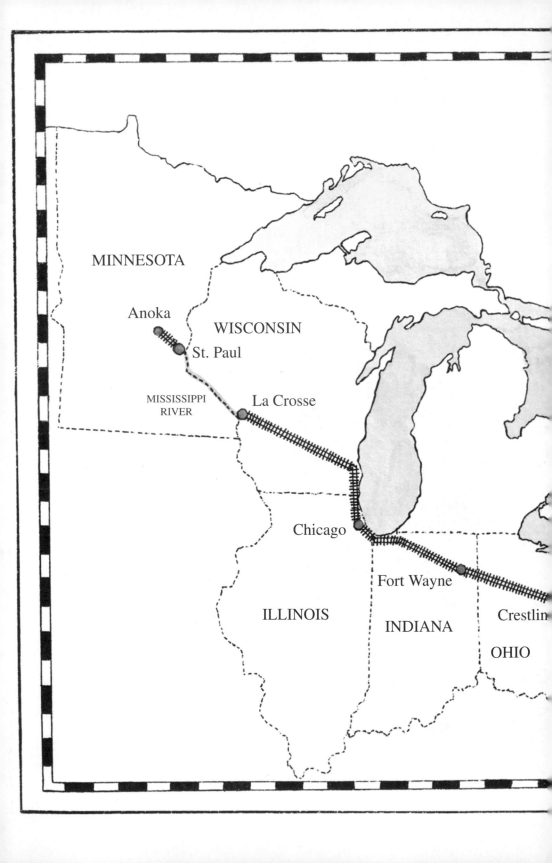

THE
LONG WAY
WESTWARD

JOAN SANDIN

PENNSYLVANIA

Pittsburgh

New York

Philadelphia

HARPER

An Imprint of HarperCollinsPublishers

For my parents

and with special thanks
to Donald Ginter

I Can Read Book® is a trademark of HarperCollins Publishers.

The Long Way Westward. Copyright © 1989 by Joan Sandin. All rights reserved. Manufactured in China. No part of this book may be used or reproduced in any manner whatsoever without written permission except in the case of brief quotations embodied in critical articles and reviews. For information address HarperCollins Children's Books, a division of HarperCollins Publishers, 195 Broadway, New York, NY 10007.

Library of Congress Control Number: 89-2024
ISBN 978-0-06-025207-6 (lib. bdg.)—ISBN 978-0-06-444198-8 (pbk.)

16 17 18 19 20 SCP 24 23 22 ❖

CONTENTS

I. THE NEW LAND

"Look, Carl Erik," said Jonas,
"the streets of America
are not paved with gold."

"Oh, Jonas!" said Carl Erik.

He smiled at his little brother.

"That is just something people say.
It means America is a rich land."
"Will we be rich?" asked Jonas.

"Maybe not rich," said their father,
"but we will never eat bark bread,
as we did in Sweden."

After twelve days
on an emigrant boat,
it felt good to be on land again.
But New York was not for them.
It was big and crowded and noisy.

Whistles blew, people shouted.

A train rumbled over their heads.

"Thank God we are not staying here,"

said Mamma.

She hugged the baby tighter.

The cart stopped at a busy pier.

They were packed onto a ferryboat.

Mamma looked

across the Hudson River

at the green hills of New Jersey.

How much longer to Minnesota?

she wondered.

"ATTENTION, COUNTRYMEN!"

shouted the railroad agent.

"Your trunks are checked through.

You are on your own, now.

There is the emigrant train.

You must change in Philadelphia.

Does anyone know English?

No?

Well, just show your tickets, then.

The train stops often.

Keep an eye on your children.

Be calm and stay together."

Carl Erik and Jonas

ran ahead of the others.

They climbed aboard the train.

It was warm inside.

Gas lamps lit the car.

"Oh, Carl Erik!"

whispered Jonas.

He touched the red plush seats.

"This must be the king's train!"

"There is no king in America,"

said Carl Erik.

"In America,

everybody travels like this."

"WHAT ARE YOU TWO

DOING IN HERE!"

cried an angry voice.

"RUN!"

Carl Erik told Jonas.

17

They ran through the car,

down the steps,

and out onto the platform.

18

The railroad agent laughed.

"What were you doing in first class?

Here is where you belong, boys."

Their car was crowded,
dark, and cold.
It had wooden benches,
a water bucket, and a coal stove.
Their first night in America,
they slept on the floor.

"PHILADELPHIA!"

shouted the conductor.

"Wake up, boys!" said Pappa.

"We have to change here."

Out on the dark platform

whistles blew,

conductors shouted.

Trains were coming and going.

"Which train do we take?"

Carl Erik asked his father.

Pappa did not answer.

He looked lost and helpless.

A porter came over to them.

"Emigrant train," he said, pointing.

Carl Erik and Jonas stared at him.

They had never seen a black person.

II. ROLLING WESTWARD

A rooster crowed.

Jonas woke up and looked around.

The sun was up

over a field of corn.

"Are we in Minnesota?" he asked.

"No," said Carl Erik,

"we are in Pennsylvania—

somewhere near this big river."

He showed Jonas on the map.

Pappa rapped at the window.

"Come outside, boys!" he called.

"Come smell this rich farmland!

Look at the big barns and fields!"

"Look at the cows!" cried Jonas.

"Everything is bigger in America!"

"Will our homestead in Minnesota

be like this?" asked Carl Erik.

Pappa looked at his wife and sons.

"If we work hard," he said.

"It was not easy to leave Sweden.

Here in America,

we have a chance for a better life."

The emigrant train bumped and swayed

across the state of Pennsylvania—

past farms, factories, coal mines,

rivers, and woodlands.

"Look, Anders,"

Mamma said to Pappa,

"birch trees, just like in Sweden!"

The train moved so slowly

that Carl Erik and Jonas got out

and ran alongside the tracks.

"Look at me, Mamma!" shouted Jonas.

"I can go faster than the train!"

"Get back in here!" cried Mamma.

"How would we ever find you

if you got left behind?"

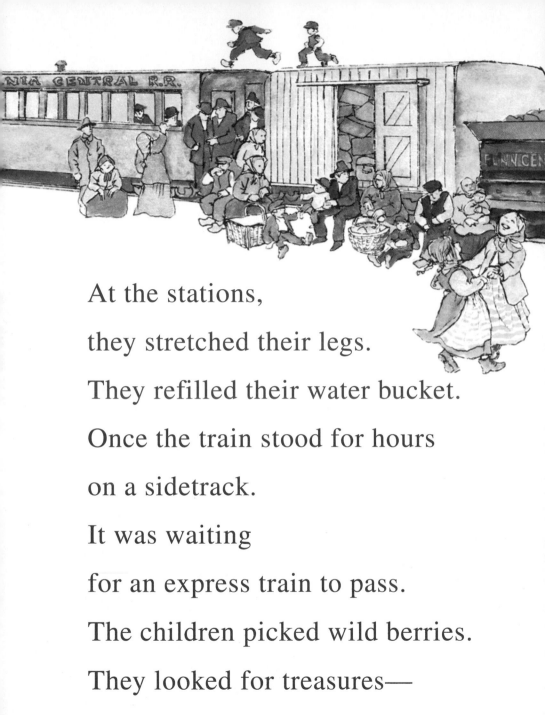

At the stations,

they stretched their legs.

They refilled their water bucket.

Once the train stood for hours

on a sidetrack.

It was waiting

for an express train to pass.

The children picked wild berries.

They looked for treasures—

pretty rocks, feathers, snails.

Jonas found a brass button.

It had a picture of a train on it.

"A conductor's button!"

he cried happily.

"Look, Pappa," said Carl Erik.

"They are serving dinner inside."

"I know," said his father,

"but it is too expensive for us.

It costs twenty-five cents."

Pappa bought milk, bread, apples,
and meat from a food seller instead.

Mamma waited her turn for the stove.

The car was thick with smoke

and cooking smells.

Hungry children

hung on their mothers' skirts.

"Women take their work with them,"

said a man with rough hands.

"I hate having nothing to do."

"Not me," said his son.

"I like being free from chores."

Carl Erik nodded.

He knew he would have lots to do

on their homestead in Minnesota.

"Where are you going?"

Carl Erik asked the boy.

"Trade Lake, Wisconsin," he said.

"Many people from our village

are already there.

I will not have to learn English."

"Our cousin in Minnesota

speaks English," said Jonas,

"and she has seen an Indian."

CLANG CLANG CLANG CLANG

The train was slowing down.

The boys saw lights ahead.

"PITTSBURGH!"

shouted the conductor.

He pushed them rudely out the door.

The Chicago express

was boarding on the next track.

But they could not get on it.

Express trains did not have
emigrant cars.

They had to wait until the next day.

In the morning,

they boarded the local train.

"There are no seats," said Mamma.

"But we have windows," said Pappa.

"Some cars have no windows."

The train rolled westward,

from Pennsylvania into Ohio.

It stopped at every station.

The men looked out the windows

at the towns and farms.

They talked about weather and crops

and the new American farm machines.

They passed around letters and maps.

"My brother Axel says

the best land is in Minnesota,"

said Pappa.

"And the climate suits us Swedes."

"There is work in Chicago,"

said a young man.

"I can earn three times

what I made in Sweden.

In America, everyone is equal.

There are no lords or kings."

Carl Erik thought about the train

with the red plush seats.

III. CHICAGO

In Crestline, Ohio,

they slept on the station floor.

They left the next morning

on the local train to Chicago.

Crestline,

Fort Wayne,

Chicago—

Carl Erik found them on the map.

"We are in Indiana now," he said.

He drew a line from town to town.

"We may reach Chicago tonight,"

Pappa told Mamma.

"Chicago is full of pickpockets

and runners," said Mamma.

"What are runners?" asked Jonas.

"They are bad men," said Pappa.

"They rob and fool newcomers."

Jonas smiled.

Nobody would rob and fool Pappa.

Pappa had their money

sewn into his coat lining.

"CHICAGO! EVERYBODY OUT!"

They got off the train.

The runners were waiting for them.

"BOARDING HOUSE!

MONEY CHANGE!"

they called out in Swedish.

A runner grabbed Mamma's bundle.

"Come with me," he said, smiling.

"There are no more trains today."

"DROP THAT BUNDLE!"

shouted a deep voice.

"BIG CARLSON!" cried the runner.

He dropped Mamma's bundle
and ran back into the crowd.
"THAT SWINE!" shouted Big Carlson.
"Trying to fool his own countrymen!"

Big Carlson held out his hand.

"I am from the Svea Society.

Our members are Chicago Swedes.

We are here to help you."

Pappa looked relieved.

"We are on our way to Minnesota.

Can you help us find our train?"

"Follow me," said Big Carlson.

He gave Mamma a folded newspaper.

"It is in Swedish," he told her.

"Inside is something sweet

for the little Swedes."

"Oh, thank you!" said Mamma.

"LA CROSSE!" cried the conductor.

"La Crosse, Wisconsin," said Pappa.

"We change to a steamboat here."

"A steamboat!" cried Carl Erik.

"Then that is the Mississippi River.

On the other side is MINNESOTA!

We are almost there!"

IV. UP THE MISSISSIPPI

The steamboat chugged upriver.

It stopped at every landing.

Its whistle

echoed through the valley.

Up on the open deck,

Carl Erik and Jonas

huddled together to kccp warm.

They heard music and laughter

from the first-class cabin below.

Early the next morning,

they landed at St. Paul, Minnesota.

"Now we must find the train

to Anoka, Minnesota," said Pappa.

"Axel is waiting for us there."

Carl Erik took out his handbook.

"Please, sir, where is the station?"

he asked a man selling cranberries.

The man laughed.

"Just follow the carts, countryman,"

he said in Swedish.

"ANOKA NEXT!"

called the conductor.

Pappa jumped off the train.

"ANDERS!" shouted a bearded man.

The two brothers

threw their arms around each other.

A young girl watched shyly.

"Anna Stina!" said Mamma.

"How you have grown

these last two years!"

"If you are Anna Stina," said Jonas,

"then this is for you."

He held out his conductor's button.

"Come!" said Uncle Axel.

"Sara is waiting for us.

We can be home before dark."

"Home!" said Mamma with a sigh.

"Home!"

The long journey was over.

They were finally home.

Home in their new land—

America!

AUTHOR'S NOTE

During the "hunger years" of 1868 and '69, more than 50,000 Swedish emigrants* landed on America's shores. Most went westward to free homestead lands. Many settled in Minnesota.

Their journey was hard. They were packed into so-called "emigrant cars" attached to slow trains, the worst the railroads had to offer. They did not speak English, and the many changes, delays, and sidetrackings were impossible for them to understand. Crews were often rude and there were many accidents.

Thousands of new arrivals were helped by the Swedish community, through the churches and clubs such as the Svea Society in Chicago.

---

* An *emigrant* is someone who leaves his own country to live in a new one. After he arrives he is called an *immigrant*. These words have often been confused and used incorrectly. For instance, the train the immigrants rode was commonly but incorrectly called the *emigrant train*.